LOVED TO BITS

For Ben —Teresa Heapy

For my father, whose childhood adventures
helped inspire these drawings —Katie Cleminson

Text copyright © 2018 by Teresa Heapy
Illustrations copyright © 2018 by Katie Cleminson
Published by Roaring Brook Press
Roaring Brook Press is a division of Holtzbrinck Publishing Holdings Limited Partnership
175 Fifth Avenue, New York, NY 10010
mackids.com

Library of Congress Control Number: 2018935591
ISBN: 978-1-250-18694-2

Our books may be purchased in bulk for promotional, educational, or business use.
Please contact your local bookseller or the Macmillan Corporate and Premium Sales Department
at (800) 221-7945 ext. 5442 or by e-mail at MacmillanSpecialMarkets@macmillan.com.

First American edition, 2018
Published in the United Kingdom by David Fickling Books
Printed in China by Toppan Leefung Printing Ltd., Dongguan City, Guangdong Province

1 3 5 7 9 10 8 6 4 2

LOVED

TO BITS

Teresa Heapy & Katie Cleminson

Roaring Brook Press

New York

My teddy's special.
Stripy Ted.

He's not allowed
to leave my bed.

For long ago, he was . . .

. . . a super, somersaulting Ted,

all golden stripes
from foot to head,

who made adventures
around my bed
from dreams we had,
and books we read.

We foiled the plot,

we fought the beast,

we rode,

we hid, we found the feast.

We tickled
monsters,

fled on rafts,

we searched,

explored,

escaped . . .

and laughed.

And if I stumbled,
back he sped
to rescue me,
with arms outspread.

"Take my paw . . .

and
ONWARD!"

said my furry,
funny, fearless Ted.

There was the time
he tumbled

SPLOSH!

Terrific
stuff!
I love a wash!

There was the
time he lost
an ear—

Still got
the best one—
never fear!

And then the time his eye went

PING!

"It's nothing! Didn't feel a thing!"

And once, within a tug-of-war . . .

And once, his leg got tangled

. . . thump!

...he slipped.

I caught
his paw.

I held him
tightly

just

once

more.

But

in the end . . .

the

last

stitch

tore

and

Stripy Ted

fell

to

the

floor.

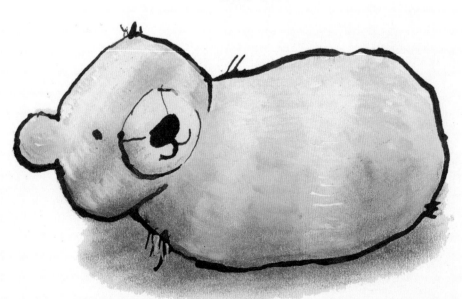

I picked him up.

A scruffy Ted.

No arms and legs—
just hanging threads.

Golden stripes
now brown instead.

Battered,

worn-out

ball and head.

Mom reached for him.

"Poor little Ted.
Shall I mend him?"

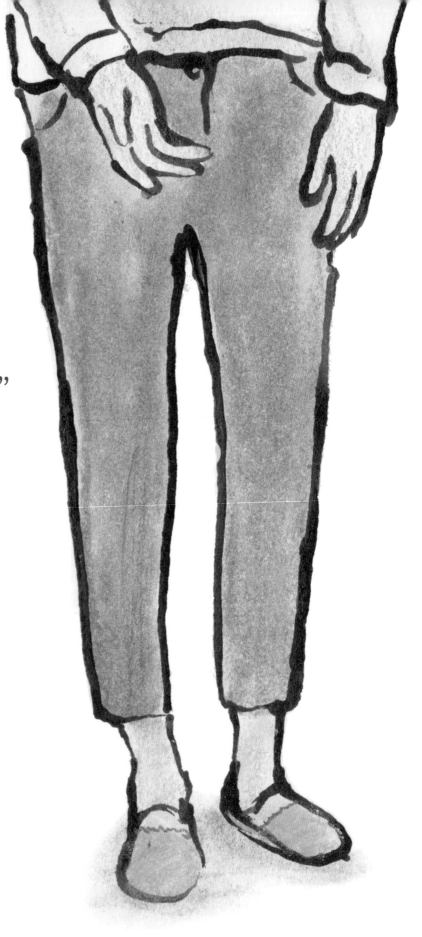

"No," I said.

The truth
was now,

I liked him better.

I could hold him in one hand.

He fit right,

just here.

He knows my hopes,
my secret schemes,

my stories,
wishes,
fears and
dreams.

Yes, my teddy's special.
Stripy Ted.

And he belongs with me in bed.